The BLUES Go Birding
at Wild America's Shores

Meet the BLUES

BING

Band Leader

Favorite color: Maroon

Bing loves:
- singing songs
- rhyming words
- using maps

Favorite expression:

"Let's cruise, BLUES!"

LULU

Blue Belle

Favorite color: Pink

Lulu loves:
- dressing up
- making friends
- taking photos

Favorite expression:

"Think pink!"

UNO

One-of-a-kind

Favorite color: Orange

Uno loves:
- playing the guitar
- loons and rubber duckies
- and not much else

Favorite expression:

"Uh-oh!"

EGGBERT

Super Birder

Favorite color: Green

Eggbert loves
- watching birds
- reading about birds
- talking about birds

Favorite expression:

"Birding is the best!"

SAMMI

Sportster

Favorite color: Yellow

Sammi loves
- doing ALL sports
- getting a good workout
- going on adventures

Favorite expression:

"Girl power!"

By Carol L. Malnor and Sandy F. Fuller ✳ Illustrated by Louise Schroeder

DAWN PUBLICATIONS

With appreciation to RTP. — CLM

For W. Ellsworth, who always knew The BLUES would fly, with much love. — SFF

For my parents, Wilfrid and Eve Labrecque of Saskatoon, Saskatchewan, Canada. — LS

ACKNOWLEDGEMENTS

Wild America by Roger Tory Peterson and James Fisher and *Return to Wild America: A Yearlong Search for the Continent's Natural Soul* by Scott Weidensaul provided the inspiration for the BLUES' second journey and also determined the destinations and selection of birds included in the book.

The authors are especially grateful to the following people for helping the BLUES continue their birding adventures: Glenn Hovemann and Muffy Weaver for their creative and editorial skills; Joseph, Suzanne, Camille, and Sophie Schroeder for their valuable "constructive criticism" and imaginative suggestions; and Barbara Herkert for the use of her beautiful United States map.

Special thanks go to Andrea Yocum and her 2009-2010 first-grade students at Yuba Environmental Science Charter Academy in Oregon House, California, and Karen Busch and her 2009-2010 first- through third-grade students at Living Wisdom School, Portland, Oregon.

We are grateful to the following bird experts for their assistance in assuring the accuracy of bird facts: Anne James-Rosenberg, Gary Langham, Ed Pandolfino, Scott Weidensaul, and Julie Zickefoose. Important sources for bird information used in this book include *All About Birds* (Cornell Lab of Ornithology: www.allaboutbirds.org) and *The Birds of North America Online* (Cornell Lab of Ornithology and the American Ornithologists' Union: http://bna.birds.cornell.edu).

LIBRARY OF CONGRESS CATALOGING-IN-PUBLICATION DATA

Malnor, Carol.

The Blues go birding at Wild America shores / by Carol L. Malnor and Sandy F. Fuller ; illustrated by Louise Schroeder. -- 1st ed.

  p. cm.

 Summary: Following in the footsteps of famed birder Roger Tory Peterson, five little birds go on a birdwatching trip around North America's shoreline and spot such shorebirds as puffins, egrets, herons, gulls, pelicans, and loons. Includes facts about Peterson and the birds encountered, online sources for listening to birdcalls, and information about the Cornell Lab citizen science project.

 Includes bibliographical references.

 ISBN 978-1-58469-131-0 (hardback) -- ISBN 978-1-58469-132-7 (pbk.) [1.

Shore birds--Fiction. 2. Birds--Fiction. 3. Bird watching--Fiction. 4. Voyages and travels--Fiction. 5. Peterson, Roger Tory, 1908-1996--Fiction.]
I. Fuller, Sandy Ferguson. II. Schroeder, Louise, ill. III. Title.

PZ7.M29635Bl 2010

[Fic]--dc22

2010010187

Manufactured by Regent Publishing Services, Hong Kong, Printed May, 2010, in ShenZhen, Guangdong, China

10 9 8 7 6 5 4 3 2 1
First Edition

Book design and computer producton by Patty Arnold, *Menagerie Design and Publishing*

DAWN PUBLICATIONS

12402 Bitney Springs Road

Nevada City, CA 95959

530-274-7775

nature@dawnpub.com

We're the BLUES! We're a band of birds who like to sing. Uno plays guitar.
On our last trip we discovered how cool it is to go bird watching.
We told everyone about it! Then a postcard arrived from Rosie,
our biggest fan in England.

Dear Bing, Lulu, Uno, Eggbert, and Sammi,
Wow! You BLUES are brilliant! I loved reading
about your trip across America to find a new song.
You heard so many birds. Did you really almost get
run over by a roadrunner?
Where are you going next? Please send me lots of
postcards, OK? Cheerio!
Your biggest fan,
Rosie Robin

THE BLUES
The Clubhouse
Songbird Lan
Hometown, U

THE BLUES

The Queen
wears pink
too!

Look at that
fancy English
stamp.

We've got
mail!

"So where *are* we going next, BLUES?"
asked Sammi. "I'm ready to rock and roll!"

Back in our Clubhouse, we wondered where to go for our next adventure. Eggbert had been reading *Wild America*, about the greatest bird watching trip ever.

I'm Lulu with my pink camera. Smile!

Uno here. I'm loony about loons.

Eggbert's my name. Birding's my game.

Sammi here, ready to sail.

"I've got it!" said Eggbert. "Let's follow in the footsteps of Roger Tory Peterson!"

"WHO?" everyone asked at once.

Eggbert explained that Peterson was a world-famous birder. In 1953 he took a trip with a friend from England. They went all around the shoreline of North America—30,000 miles in 100 days! Bing quickly pulled out his map.

"Perfect! I'll take photos!" chirped Lulu. "And we can send Rosie postcards."

Uno strummed his guitar. "Will we see a loon this time?" he grumbled.

Eggbert checked his list. "Good chance, Uno. We're going to lots of places where loons live. Peterson started in Newfoundland, Canada. So we will too."

Eggbert's Bird Note
The shore includes many different habitats. There are rocky cliffs, sandy beaches, saltwater marshes, and offshore islands. Birds have different types of wings, legs, feet, and beaks to help them live in a variety of shoreline habitats.

Eggbert's Checklist—Places to Stop!
☐ Newfoundland, Canada
☐ S. Monomoy Island, MA
☐ Chesapeake Bay, MD
☐ Merritt Island, FL
☐ Everglades, FL
☐ Dry Tortugas Islands, FL
☐ Avery Island, LA
☐ Lydia Ann Island, TX
☐ Isla Coronado, Mexico
☐ Pt. Lobos, CA
☐ Destruction Island, WA
☐ Pribilof Islands, AK

I'm Bing. When you hear my whistle blow, it's time to go.

FIELD GUIDE

WHO IS ROGER TORY PETERSON?

Roger Tory Peterson (1908-1996) was born in New York. As a young boy he loved to go bird watching in the woods and fields near his home. When he grew up he wrote *A Field Guide to the Birds* and became one of the most famous bird watchers in the world. During his "Wild America" trip with British friend James Fisher, he saw over 600 different types of birds.

Icebergs! They were floating in the ocean as we
landed in foggy Newfoundland. Peterson's friend from England had
a tricky plane landing in the fog here too.

"L-L-Looookkk!" shivered Lulu, "P-P-Penguin."

"No penguins here, Lulu—that's an Atlantic Puffin," corrected
Eggbert. "Watch him dive into that freezing water for fish!
His nickname is the 'clown of the sea' because of his colorful beak."

"Uno! I think I see a loon," called Bing. We looked and looked, but
the fog was getting thick. When we heard Bing's whistle we had to fly on,
while we still could.

"Dark rain clouds over Cape Cod!" warned Eggbert. "Good thing our island is just ahead!"

"Down quick! Pull your lines, everyone!" shouted Sammi. "Hey, what's that bird?"

"Good eye, Sammi! It's a Roseate Tern!" shouted Eggbert. "Very rare. Watch closely. It's a speedy, swooping flyer and plunge-diver."

"OOOoh, I gotta get a picture!" squealed Lulu.

That night we camped near the old lighthouse. Uno stayed up late watching its flashing beam.

Eggbert's Bird Note
The Roseate Tern's sleek wings and body allow it to make steep, fast dives into the water. It grabs fish feeding near the surface with its pointed bill.

Turn this way, tern! Smile!

Feet first, not beak!

POST CARD

Monomoy NWR, Massachusetts: A place for migratory birds to rest, eat, and nest.

Hi Rosie,

We're at a national wildlife refuge—a safe place for birds. Roseate Terns love it here during the spring and summer! Did you know that "roseate" means "pink"? These terns wear just a hint of pink feathers now that it's spring. So stylish!

Lots of love, Lulu

P.S. How did you get your pink name?

FIELD GUIDE
ROSEATE TERN
Body size: 12–14 in.
Wingspan: About 30 in.
Habitat: Ocean islands or beaches.
Food: Small ocean fish.
Sound: Sharp, high-pitched *chi-vik* or *ki-rik*.

We left Massachusetts at sunrise for the Chesapeake Bay. Hundreds of thousands of birds live here! Peterson once lived near the bay too.

Our boots went schloop! schlop! as we slogged through the mud and onto an oyster reef. An American Oystercatcher was hammering for a shellfish breakfast. "Oysters have tough shells," Eggbert announced, "but this bird's strong beak can pry into almost any shell."

Uno harrumphed. "Keep him away from my guitar."

After a messy day in the mud, Bing blew his whistle and called, "Enough trucking in the muck! Let's cruise, BLUES!"

We followed the Atlantic Flyway to Florida's eastern shore. Eggbert told us there wasn't a wildlife refuge *or* a famous space center here when Peterson visited—just birds.

"It's still a great birding spot. We might even see a flying astronaut!" Uno joked.

HA HA HA HA HA HA HA!

"That Laughing Gull thinks you're really funny," said Eggbert. "But guard your sandwich. He'll steal from anyone who's gullible—*ha*, *ha*, get it?—and laugh while he does it!"

"After lunch, we launch," announced Bing. "Ready, BLUES? 5-4-3-2-1 LIFTOFF!"

POST CARD

Merritt Island NWR, Florida: This refuge is part of NASA's Kennedy Space Center.

Hey Rosie,

You've heard of the Space Shuttle, right? Well, we're really close to where it takes off! Lots of Laughing Gulls are orbiting around too. But I'm keeping my eye on them. I just saw one rob a fish from a tern.

Lifting off,

Uno

FIELD GUIDE

LAUGHING GULL

Body size: 15-18 in.

Wingspan: 39-47 in.

Habitat: Marshes, beaches, and islands along the coast.

Food: Fish, invertebrates, insects, and garbage.

Sound: A loud series of laughing notes.

Staying close to Florida's shoreline, we soon splashed down in the warm, wet world of Everglades National Park—one of Peterson's favorite birding spots. The place looked familiar.

"Hey, isn't this near where we saw the big, *pink* Roseate Spoonbill on our last trip?" asked Lulu. "Wish I'd taken a picture of her."

"SHHHhh! Look!" said Eggbert. "It's not a big pink bird, but a great *blue* one—the Great Blue Heron. The largest heron in North America."

"I remember these mosquitoes!" said Uno, swatting. "Let's bug out!"

"Sail away, Mateys!" sang Sammi.

Eggbert's Bird Note

The Great Blue Heron is an expert at fishing. It slowly wades through the water on long legs, spreading out its toes for support in the mud. It uses its strong bill like tongs to grab a fish or frog.

POST CARD

Everglades NP, Florida: This national park is also called "The River of Grass."

Dear Rosie Robin,

I'm in Birders' Paradise! There are over 360 different kinds of birds here! With so much water and grass, these marshes are ideal places for long-legged wading birds like the Great Blue Heron.

Don't tell Uno, but more insects live in this park than birds.

Yours truly,

Eggbert

FIELD GUIDE

GREAT BLUE HERON

Body size: 38-54 in.

Wingspan: 65-79 in.

Habitat: Along calm, freshwater shorelines and seacoasts.

Food: Mainly fish; also invertebrates, amphibians, reptiles, and small mammals.

Sound: Deep, hoarse croak.

We sailed west from the Everglades into the Gulf of Mexico. "Dry Tortugas Islands, dead ahead!" sang Skipper Sammi. Just like Peterson, the first thing we saw was the tall lighthouse.

Suddenly a large shadow passed overhead. A huge bird zoomed down and attacked a gull! The frightened gull dropped its fish, and the other bird snatched it up in mid-air.

"Robbery on the high seas! Payback time for greedy gulls!" said Bing.

"Watch the Magnificent Frigatebird in action— that's why it's also called 'Man-o'-War Bird'!" exclaimed Eggbert.

"I got a picture!" chirped Lulu. "Let's sail on!"

Eggbert's Bird Note

The Magnificent Frigatebird spends most of its life soaring over the ocean. Its long wings and forked tail make it an excellent, graceful flier.

POST CARD

Dry Tortugas NP, Florida: "Dry" means there's no fresh water here. "Tortugas" is Spanish for turtles.

Ahoy, Rosie!

These islands are famous for stories about pirate ships and sunken gold. But the only "pirates" we've seen are the Magnificent Frigatebirds flying high.

The males on shore are trying to impress the females by blowing up their throat pouches like bright red balloons.

Setting sail,

Skipper Sammi

I spy . . .

. . . with only one eye. Aaargh!

FIELD GUIDE

MAGNIFICENT FRIGATEBIRD

Body size: 40 in.
Wingspan: 90 in.
Habitat: Rocky coasts of the North Atlantic and open ocean.
Food: Small fish, crustaceans, and mollusks.
Sound: Call is a growl; in the colony makes clicking, wheezy, and grating calls.

"Welcome to Bird City," announced Eggbert as we docked in Louisiana. "See all these Snowy Egrets? Long ago they were hunted almost to extinction for their lovely feathers. We can thank one man, Mr. Ned, for caring. He loved the egrets and was sad they were disappearing. So he raised and protected eight young birds. Now there are thousands."

"Hooray for Mr. Ned!" cheered Lulu. "He saved something truly beautiful. Look at their pretty white feathers and cute yellow feet!"

"Time to go to the next island," whistled Bing. "Let's wing it, BLUES!"

Snowy Egrets wade along the shoreline hunting for food. Using their bright yellow feet, they stir up the muddy bottom and scare their prey into view. Then they quickly grab it with their long bills.

POST CARD

Avery Island, Louisiana: Home to Bird City, a private bird refuge.

Howdy, Rosie,

You would love Bird City! It has beautiful gardens surrounded by winding waterways.

Peterson called this "The Flying Gardens of Avery Island" because birds are in the air everywhere.

Thousands of Snowy Egrets come here to nest every spring. So do many tourists, just to see them. Isn't it cool that people are taking good care of the birds?

Winging away,

Bing

Ooh! I like their cute, yellow boots!

Those are their feet, Lulu, not boots.

FIELD GUIDE

SNOWY EGRET

Body size: 22-26 in.

Wingspan: 41-45 in.

Habitat: Ponds, marshes, ocean shorelines.

Food: Wide variety including fish, worms, insects, snails, frogs, and snakes.

Sound: A loud squawk.

son got caught in a fierce storm as he traveled along the Gulf Coast of Texas and so did we! rybody OK?" asked Eggbert, shaking off.

ucky for us the lighthouse showed the way," said Uno. "Hey, check out all those little busybodies."

We splashed in the waves among dozens of skittering shorebirds—
Sanderlings, Willets, and Whimbrels—all members of the Sandpiper family.
They were looking for food. We were just playing!

Finally Bing asked, "Are we dry enough to fly? It's a long way to our next stop."

Eggbert's Bird Note

Sanderlings have short legs and bills. They peck for food at the water's edge. With their longer legs, Willets can go farther out into the water. Whimbrels probe in the sand with curved bills that are the same shape as a crab's burrow.

POST CARD

Lydia Ann Island, Texas: One of many barrier islands along the Texas coastline.

Hi, Roz!

When we arrived here it looked like a Sandpiper Family Reunion. Shorebirds of all shapes and sizes were everywhere! Long legs and short legs were running along the water. Straight beaks and curved beaks were poking in the sand. What fun! I snapped a family portrait.

Luv U, ♥ Lulu

P.S. Wish you were here so we could have a BLUES FANS Reunion.

FIELD GUIDE

SANDPIPER FAMILY

Habitat: Shorelines.
Food: Invertebrates, like snails, worms, and crabs.
Sanderling Body size: 7 in.
Willet Body size: 15 in.
Whimbrel Body size: 17 in.

We flew over Mexico on our long flight to an island in the Pacific.

As we glided down, Uno gasped, "IS THAT A LOON??"

Eggbert shook his head. "Close, but it's actually a Brandt's Cormorant. Both loons and cormorants dive underwater to catch fish. But only cormorants hang their wings out to dry."

Peterson camped here, but not us. Way too rocky. "Adios, cormorant!" We sang together as we headed north, "California here we come."

Eggbert's Bird Note

Unlike terns and pelicans that plunge from the air, cormorants dive from the surface of the ocean. They swim powerfully underwater with their feet and grab fish with their hooked bills.

POST CARD

Isla Coronado, Mexico: Desolate island in the Pacific near the U.S. border.

Buenos Dias, Señorita Rosa!

We're on a rocky island in Mexico. I REALLY thought I saw a loon, but nope. It was a Brandt's Cormorant. After diving for fish he had to dry his waterlogged feathers in the sun and wind.

At least I saw another lighthouse! That makes number four.

Hasta la vista,

Uno the Birdito

FIELD GUIDE

BRANDT'S CORMORANT

Body size: 34 in.

Wingspan: 48 in.

Habitat: Inshore coastal waters, especially where there are kelp beds.

Food: Fish and squid.

Sound: Mostly silent; call is a low croak.

Floating along the California coast, we came to a bed of kelp seaweed at Point Lobos. "I'm not sure I like it here," peeped Lulu. "Doesn't 'lobos' mean WOLVES? I hear howling!"

"You're safe," chuckled Eggbert. "Those are sea lions barking. Heads up! A Brown Pelican!"

A graceful bird plunged into the ocean, scooped up a fish in its pouch, quickly swallowed it, and landed on the rocks.

"Now that guy knows how to fish," sang Sammi.

"Air pressure check, BLUES," said Bing. "Time to float to our next stop."

Look! Sea lions!

POST CARD

Pt. Lobos State Natural Reserve, California: Often called the greatest meeting of land and sea.

Dear Rosie Robin,

Peterson wrote that Point Lobos looked like "a three-ringed circus." I agree! There's so much to see and hear—sea lions barking on the rocks, otters floating around kelp beds, and Brown Pelicans diving for fish.

The pelican's pouch can hold up to 25 pounds of fish and water. That's a lot more than our fishing nets.

Sincerely,

Eggbert

FIELD GUIDE

BROWN PELICAN

Body size: 39-54 in.

Wing span: 78-84 in.

Habitat: Warm ocean coasts.

Food: Mainly fish.

Sound: Usually silent.

Our leaky raft almost didn't make it all the way to Destruction Island. But Uno lit up when he spotted another lighthouse.

"Perfect timing to run out of air," said Eggbert. "Now listen for the energetic song of the Winter Wren. Peterson loved this little bird's voice."

Bing was the first to hear the high-pitched notes. "What a performer! Let's jam!" Uno pulled out his guitar while the rest of us grabbed driftwood sticks and seashell rattles.

We played until sunset. Then Bing whistled. "North to Alaska, BLUES. Fly high!"

Wrens rock, *tik-tik-tik*!

Lighthouses rock, beep-bob-adoo! ♪♫

Lighthouses sure light you up, Uno!

Eggbert's Bird Note

The Winter Wren is able to live in lots of different habitats. It's found all over North America and it's the only wren that also lives in Europe, Asia, and Africa.

POST CARD

Destruction Island, Washington: Home to Quillayute Needles National Wildlife Refuge.

A note for you, Rosie, ♪

While watching seabirds on this windy island, we heard a Winter Wren. What a great singer! So full of energy, with amazing buzzes and trills. His voice sounded perfect for our band. But we knew he couldn't come with us. We're off to Alaska!

Singing all the way,

Bing

FIELD GUIDE

WINTER WREN

Body size: 3-4 1/2 in.

Wingspan: 4 1/2–6 1/2 in.

Habitat: Usually prefers forests; also lives on treeless islands off the coast.

Food: Invertebrates including insects, spiders, and millipedes.

Sound: Continuous stream of melodious notes and trills.

Our final stop—faraway Alaskan islands. Last chance to spot a loon! Birds were perched in every nook and cranny. "No wonder Peterson loved this place," said Eggbert.

"There *must* be a loon here," Uno whined.

"Loons dive for their dinner!" said Bing. "So let's go below!"

Peering through our submarine's porthole, Lulu screamed, "Uno, there's one!"

"Sorry, that's a Thick-billed Murre," said Eggbert. "See, it's swimming with its wings. Loons swim with their feet."

Uno started to cry. We tried to comfort him. But no luck. No loon.

Eggbert's Bird Note

The Thick-billed Murre's eggs are quite pointed at one end. If the egg rolls, it will go around in a circle. This shape keeps the egg from rolling off the high ledges where murres nest.

POST CARD

Pribilof Islands, Alaska: Remote islands in the Bering Sea.

Hiya, Rosie,

We made it all the way around North America following Peterson's Wild America route!

Tons of birds here! Over 220 different kinds. I loved watching Thick-billed Murres because they're such powerful underwater swimmers.

But no loon for Uno. Poor guy. We all feel really sorry for him.

Heading for home,

Sammi

FIELD GUIDE

THICK-BILLED MURRE

Body size: 17-19 in.
Wingspan: 25-28 in.
Habitat: Northern oceans.
Food: Fish.
Sound: Mostly silent.

Winging our way home over a Minnesota lake, we heard an eerie echoing call.
Ow-OOOOh, OOOh, OOOh! "I HEAR A LOON!" Eggbert shouted.

Ow-OOOOh, OOOh, OOOh! "There it is again! A Common Loon." We grabbed a canoe
to get a closer view.

"LOOOOOK! OVER THERE!" gasped Uno. "It's Mama Loon! She's carrying her
babies on her back to keep them safe. There's Daddy Loon too. OOOOH!"

"Uno, you even sound like a loon!" exclaimed Bing. And we all joined in the chorus
before happily heading home.

Eggbert's Bird Note

The Common Loon is built like a torpedo, which makes it a great diver. Sharp points on the roof of its mouth and tongue help it keep a firm hold on slippery fish.

POST CARD

Loon Lake, MN: The loon is Minnesota's State Bird.

Hey Rosie!

We saw a family of Common Loons! They have four calls. I've been practicing all of them . . . maybe I'm just a wannabe loon.

Each call is different. One sounds like a wolf howling, *Ow-OOOOh, OOOh, OOOh!* Kinda scary. Another is just a short hoot. Then there's the yodel *ow-Ah-oooo, ow-Ah-oooo.* My favorite is a crazy laugh. Now I've really heard WILD America!

UnOO-OO-OO-OO

Ow-OOOOh, OOOh, OOOh!

FIELD GUIDE

COMMON LOON

Body size: 26-36 in.
Wingspan: 40-51 in.
Habitat: Ocean coastlines (winter) and cold, freshwater lakes (summer).
Food: Mostly fish.
Sound: Wail, hoot, tremolo, and yodel.

Home again! We rested our wings and enjoyed Eggbert's popcorn as we shared Lulu's photos on our clubhouse porch.

We saw FOUR loons, Rubber Ducky!

What an adventure! BLUES gone wild!

"Just look at that Roseate Tern—so stylish! It's my favorite. What are yours?" asked Lulu.

"Nothing can top a family of loons!" Uno exclaimed. "Two babies!"

Eggbert announced, "My favorite's the Great Blue Heron—the largest heron in America."

"Mine's the Winter Wren," sighed Bing. "It was the smallest bird, but the most energetic."

"How about that Magnificent Frigatebird?" sang Sammi. "It had the biggest wingspan—over seven feet! Hey, next time let's find the bird that flies fastest, or dives deepest, or has the quickest wingbeat. Let's go EXTREME birding!"

"Maybe," said Eggbert. "But for now, let's kick back and remember WILD AMERICA."

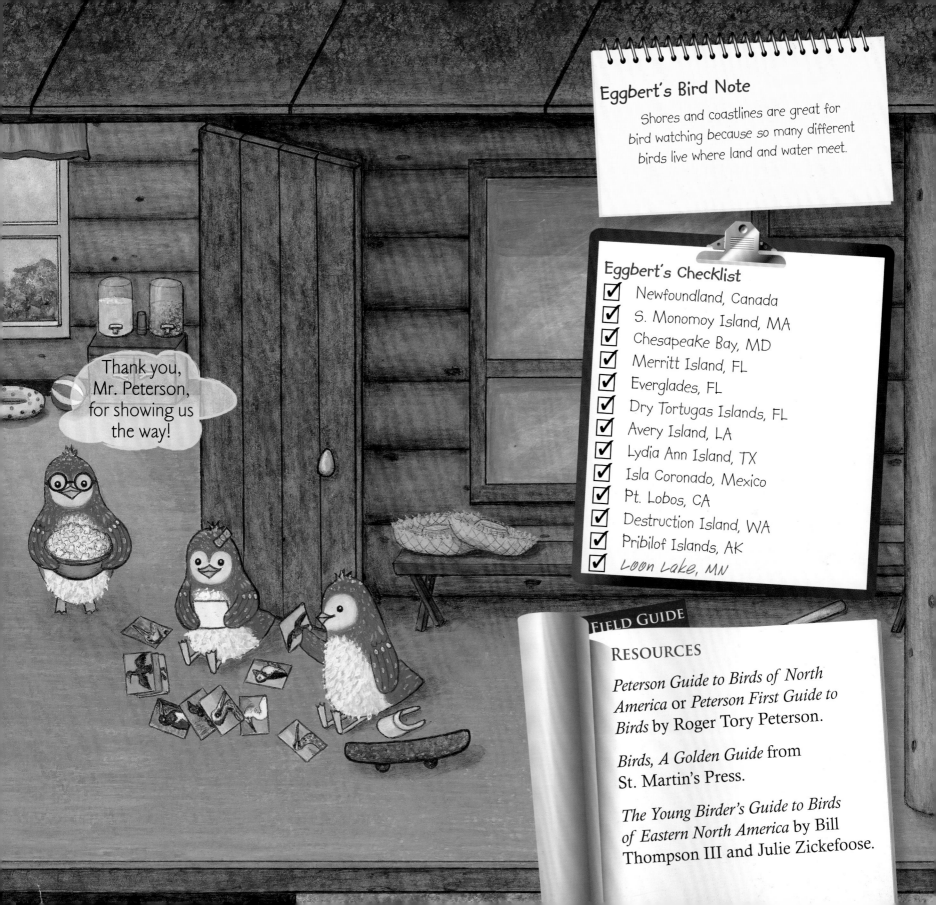

We went 30,000 miles. Just like Peterson!
Eggbert
I'm Speedy Sammi. Girl Power!
Sammi
Uh-oh, mine's just a puddle paddle!
Uno
Alaska
Yukon
Nunavit
Northwest Territories
British Columbia
Alberta
Manitoba
Saskatchewan
Ontario
Washington
North Dakota
Montana
Minnesota
Oregon
Idaho
South Dakota
Wisconsin
Wyoming
California
Nevada
Nebraska
Iowa
Illinois
Utah
Colorado
Kansas
Missouri
Arizona
New Mexico
Oklahoma
Arkansas
Mississippi
Texas
Louisiana
Mexico

Greenland

From sea to shining sea ♩ again! 🎵

Bing's Notebook

We traveled all around North America's shoreline following in Roger Tory Peterson's footsteps. We marked the places where we stopped on our map. Some places were national parks (NP) or national wildlife refuges (NWR). Some birds live at the shore year-round. Others live there only part of the year or stop at the shore during migration.

Quebec

Labrador and Newfoundland

New Brunswick — _Prince Edward Island_

Maine _Nova Scotia_

Vermont
New Hampshire
Massachusetts
New York _Rhode Island_
nsylvania _Connecticut_
Connecticut
New Jersey
Maryland
West Virginia _Delaware_
Virginia

North Carolina
South arolina

Birds and shores galore!

Birds We Saw Along the Shore

Newfoundland, Canada—**Atlantic Puffin**
Monomoy NWR, MA—**Roseate Tern**
Chesapeake Bay, MD—**American Oystercatcher**
Merritt Island NWR, FL—**Laughing Gull**
Everglades NP, FL— **Great Blue Heron**
Dry Tortugas NP, FL—**Magnificent Frigatebird**
Avery Island, LA—**Snowy Egret**
Lydia Ann Island, TX—**Sandpiper Family**
Coronado Islands, Mexico—**Brandt's Cormorant**
Pt. Lobos State Reserve, CA—**Brown Pelican**
Destruction Island, WA—**Winter Wren**
Pribolof Islands, AK—**Thick-billed Murre**
Loon Lake, MN—**Common Loon**

Have More Fun with Birds

Find interesting and fun information, projects, birding tips, resources, and curriculum for kids, teachers, and parents:

- The National Audubon Society www.audubon.org
- Cornell Lab of Ornithology www.birds.cornell.edu
- Bird Watcher's Digest www.birdwatchersdigest.com
- American Birding Assn. www.aba.org
- Birder's World www.birdersworld.com

Hear What Uno Heard

Listen to four amazing loon calls online at Journey North www.learner.org/jnorth/tm/loon/identification.html#Looney

Another great place to listen to bird songs and calls is "All About Birds", Cornell Lab's online guide to birds and bird watching. www.allaboutbirds.org Type any bird's name into the search box to hear sounds, see photographs, and read Cool Facts.

Become a Citizen Scientist

Help scientists better understand birds by joining a Cornell Lab citizen science project. www.birds.cornell.edu/netcommunity/citsci/projects

Projects include:

- Project FeederWatch—Count birds at your feeders during the winter.
- The Great Backyard Bird Count—Join a one-day, nationwide event.
- Celebrate Urban Birds!—Discover birds that live in your city.

About the Bird-Lovers Who Wrote and Illustrated This Book

CAROL L. MALNOR
Nature Book Lady

Favorite color: All shades of blue

Carol loves
- going birding
- writing books
- doing Tai Chi

Favorite expression:

"Mistakes are wonderful opportunities to learn."

Carol lives with her husband in the foothills of the Sierra Nevada, where she has breakfast with her backyard birds each morning.

SANDY F. FULLER
Kid-at-Heart

Favorite color: Blue (It's true!)

Sandy loves
- family and friends
- mountains and Maine
- guitars and gourmet

Favorite expression:

"FAR OUT!"

Sandy lives in Colorado, sharing mountain life with Riva (golden retriever), Ellsworth (aka Bill) and Scott and Kimberly (when they visit Mom!).

LOUISE SCHROEDER
World Traveler

Favorite color: Aquamarine

Louise loves
- being with family
- enjoying nature
- painting

Favorite expression:

"Let's go somewhere."

A native of rural Canada and visual creator of the Blues, Louise lives with her husband and three daughters in Las Vegas, Nevada.

THE BLUES invite parents, teachers, and kids to visit them at **www.thebluesgobirding.com**. You'll discover great birding resources, lesson plans, backyard bird watching tips, citizen science projects, coloring pages, and more.

Dawn Publications is dedicated to inspiring in children a deeper understanding and appreciation for all life on Earth. You can browse through our titles, download resources for teachers, and order at www.dawnpub.com, or call 800-545-7475.